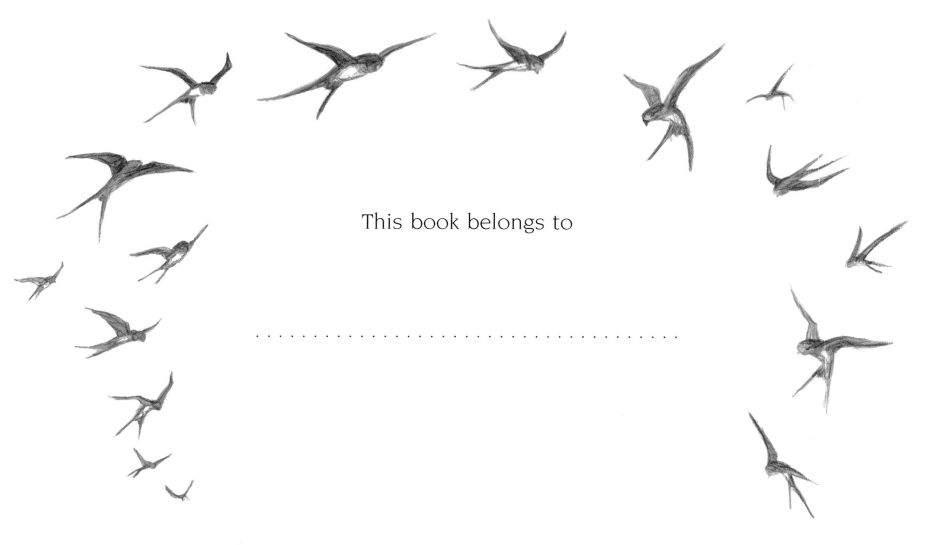

This book belongs to

. . . .

For Helen ~ J.D.

To Chus and Mila Maisie, with love ~ P.S.

EGMONT
We bring stories to life

First published in Great Britain 2007
by Egmont UK Limited
The Yellow Building, 1 Nicholas Road, London W11 4AN

Text first published in Great Britain 2000
Text copyright © Julia Donaldson 2000
Illustrations copyright © Pam Smy 2007

The author and illustrator have asserted their moral rights

ISBN 978 1 4052 1788 0 (Paperback)

A CIP catalogue record for this title is available from the British Library

www.egmont.co.uk

Stay safe online. Any website addresses listed in this book are correct at the time of going to print. However, Egmont is not responsible for content hosted by third parties. Please be aware that online content can be subject to change and websites can contain content that is unsuitable for children. We advise that all children are supervised when using the internet.

FOLLOW THE SWALLOW

Written by **Julia Donaldson**

Illustrated by **Pam Smy**

EGMONT

Chack the blackbird was learning to fly.
So was Apollo the swallow.

That was how they met.

"Hello! I'm Apollo. I'm a swallow."

"And what do you swallow?"
asked Chack.
"Flies, mostly," said Apollo.
"And who are you?"

"I'm Chack. I'm a blackbird."
"You look brown to me," said Apollo.
"I may be brown now, but one
day I'll be black," said Chack.
"I don't believe you!" said Apollo.

Apollo showed Chack his nest.
It was inside the garden shed.
"I won't always live here," he said.
"One day I'll fly away to Africa."
"I don't believe you!" said Chack.

Chack showed Apollo his nest.
It was in a tree covered in white blossom.
"One day the tree will be covered in tasty
orange berries," said Chack.
"I don't believe you!" said Apollo.

The days grew longer and warmer.
Apollo started going around
with a lot of other swallows.

They kept gathering on the roof
of the shed and then flying
off all together.

"What are you doing?" asked Chack.
"Practising flying to Africa!" said Apollo.
"I don't believe you!" said Chack.

The white blossom fell off Chack's tree
and some little green berries appeared.
"They'll be orange one day," he told Apollo.
"I don't believe you!" said Apollo.

Slowly the berries on the tree grew bigger and changed colour,

from green . . .

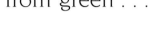

to yellow . . .

and at last to orange.

"Now Apollo will believe me!" said Chack.

He flew to the shed to tell his friend about the orange berries.
"Come to the tree! Come to the tree!" he called.

But Apollo had gone! He and the
other swallows had just set off for Africa.
Chack flew after the swallows. He flew
and he flew till he reached the sea.

There he met a jumpy dolphin.

"Can you take a message to Apollo the swallow from Chack the blackbird?" asked Chack. "He's on his way to Africa."
"What is the message?" asked the dolphin.
"**come to the tree!**" said Chack, and he flew back to eat some of the tasty orange berries.

The jumpy dolphin swam,

and leapt

and dived.

It took him a long time to reach Africa.

There the dolphin met a grumpy camel.
"Can you take a message to Apollo the
swallow from Chack the blackbird?"
asked the dolphin.

"What is the message?" asked the camel.
"Er . . . er . . . *jump in the sea!*" said the dolphin.

The grumpy camel trudged slowly
across the desert . . .

. . . till he reached a wide river.
There he met a greedy crocodile.

"Can you take a message to Apollo the swallow
from Chack the blackbird?" asked the camel.
"What is the message?" asked the crocodile.
"Er . . . er . . . '*Grumpy like me!*'" said the camel.

The greedy crocodile took his time swimming
and snapping his way down the river . . .

. . . till he came to a forest.
There he met a playful monkey.
"Can you take a message to Apollo the swallow
from Chack the blackbird?" asked the crocodile.

"What is the message?"
asked the monkey.

"Er . . . er . . . 'Monkey for tea!'" said the crocodile.

The playful monkey swung from branch
to branch until he came to a fig tree.
On the ground lay a lot of rotten figs.
Feeding on the rotten figs were a lot
of fruit flies, and snapping at the
fruit flies were a lot of swallows.

"I've got a message for Apollo
the swallow," said the monkey.
"That's me!" said one of the swallows.
"What is the message and who is it from?"

"It's from Chack the blackbird and the message is . . .
er . . . er . . . 'One, two, three, whee!'" said the monkey.

"One, two, three, whee!" said Apollo.
"That's a funny message! Well, I've been
in Africa for half a year now. It's time for
me to fly back to the garden. I can
find out what Chack means."

Apollo and the other swallows flew back over the forest . . .

and the river . . .

and the desert . . .

and the sea . . .

. . . till they reached the garden.

Apollo flew to Chack's tree.
It was covered in white blossom.
A big blackbird flew down from the tree.

"I'm looking for my
friend, Chack," said Apollo.
"That's me!" said the blackbird.

"I don't believe you!" said Apollo.
"You're black and Chack was brown."

"I'm Chack as sure as eggs are eggs,"
said Chack. "And talking of eggs,
I've got something to show you."

Chack flew up to a nest in the tree.
A brown bird was sitting in the nest.
"Time for your worm-break, Rowena,"
said Chack to the brown bird.
Rowena flew off, and there in the nest
Apollo saw three bluey-green eggs.

"So the message wasn't
'**One, two, three, whee!**' It was
'**One, two, three eggs!**'" he said.
"No it wasn't!" said Chack.
"It was '**Come to the tree!**'"

"Well, I have come to the tree and
I've seen the eggs, and I think they're
beautiful," said Apollo.

"But the message wasn't about the eggs,
it was about the orange berries," said Chack.

"Orange berries! You're not still on about orange
berries, are you?" Apollo started to laugh.

"But there really *were* orange berries!" said Chack. "I ate lots and lots of them.

"The rest fell off the tree in winter.

"But in spring there were some new buds.

"Now the white blossom is back, and in the autumn there will be some more orange berries. You *must* believe me, Apollo!"

Apollo thought hard.

"All right, then,"
he said,
"I believe you."